CHOMPS

BIGGER BITES FOR BIGGER READERS!

Stella by the Sea

Stella wants an ordinary house,
an ordinary backyard, and a dog. But her mom
Lucille is a real-estate legend and
her dad Henry is a famous TV garden expert, and
nowhere they live is ordinary.

Then one day, Stella spots
the house of her dreams and discovers
that life is full of surprises.

BIGGER BITES FOR
CHOMPS
BIGGER READERS!

Stella by the Sea

**Stella's not just an ordinary girl
in an ordinary world!**

Ruth Starke

RUNNING PRESS
KIDS
PHILADELPHIA·LONDON

For M and M

Library of Congress Control Number: 2005928816

ISBN-13: 978-0-7624-2625-6
ISBN-10: 0-7624-2625-X

Original design by David Altheim and Susannah Low, Penguin Design Studio.
Additional design for this edition by Frances J. Soo Ping Chow.

Typography: ITC Berkeley, MetaPlus, and New Century Schoolbook

This book may be ordered by mail from the publisher.
Please include $2.50 for postage and handling.
But try your bookstore first!

This edition published by Running Press Kids, an imprint of
Running Press Book Publishers
125 South Twenty-second Street
Philadelphia, Pennsylvania 19103-4399

Visit us on the web!
www.runningpress.com

Ages 8–12
Grades 3–6

chapter ✽ 1

Stella Seaton was not the sort of person who normally took much notice of dreams. But she had dreamed the same dream three times now, which didn't seem normal at all. Obviously her subconscious was trying to tell her something. Clearly it was a case for Mary Sparkel.

Mary, an expert on dreams, was in Stella's class. She had a book which gave the meaning of every dream in the world. Or so Mary claimed, and so far nobody had come up with one to stump her. Stella wasn't sure she quite believed everything Mary said, but last week Jade O'Leary had gone to her with a dream about riding a zebra up Mount Everest.

"The climbing and the snow both mean wealth," Mary had told her. "The zebra indicates confusion, so you're soon going to get a lot of money you won't know what to do with. Fifty cents please."

Since she was about to be rich, Jade had paid up cheerfully, even though she knew she wouldn't be confused at all. "I know exactly what I'm going to buy," she confided to Stella. "I've been saving up all year for a pair of black leather boots."

The very next day, Jade received a birthday card from her grandfather with a fifty-dollar bill inside. Wow, she thought. Mary Sparkel had predicted wealth and here it was.

The day after that she got another birthday card from her grandfather and another fifty dollars. This was getting a little strange. She showed her mother. "Even if it was my birthday, which it's not, why is Grandpa sending me two cards and two sums of money?"

Her mother had sighed. "He's getting old. Old people sometimes get confused. Just write and thank him."

So Mary Sparkel had been doubly right! Jade, and indeed everyone in the class, had been totally impressed. "You were so right about my dream," Jade told Mary. "Except it wasn't me who was confused, it was my grandpa."

"Whatever," said Mary Sparkel.

Yes, Stella thought, Mary Sparkel would certainly know what her dream meant. And luckily, it being an unusually slow week for dreams, she was granted an immediate appointment. When Mary was in high demand, you had to wait in line, sometimes for days.

At morning recess, they sat down together in a quiet corner of the playground. Mary placed her

Dream Decoder on her knees and tapped it with her pencil. "Go ahead," she said, sounding and looking very professional.

Stella cleared her throat. "Okay. So here's my dream. I'm walking along this street. Just an ordinary street. And I come to a sweet little house made of gingerbread—"

"Gingerbread?" Mary flicked to *G* in her dream book.

"Yes. Just like those little gingerbread houses you see at Christmas, decorated with candies and licorice and white squiggly icing. The garden of this house has little trees made of spearmint leaves and there are two rows of ripe raspberry bushes leading up to the front door. Which looks exactly like a chocolate cookie."

"That could be important. *C* for chocolate or cookie, I wonder?"

"I don't think it's important," Stella said.

"I'll be the judge of that."

"Sorry. Anyway, in the garden is a wizard."

"Wizard." Mary flicked to *W* in her dream book.

"At least, he looks like a wizard. He's an old man with long white hair and a funny sort of hat and there's a big silver star on his chest. He's got a skinny black cat—"

"Cats." Mary turned to *C* in her dream book. "Cats are always significant; especially black ones."

"It doesn't mean death or anything, does it? I mean, it seemed quite a happy cat. I'm sure it rubbed against my leg, and purred. Surely that can't be bad. *Can* it?"

"I can't possibly say until I've heard the whole dream. Context is everything."

"Right. Well, the wizard says, 'Stella, you can have one wish. What do you want most in the world?' Then he waves this sort of wand—"

"Wand!" Mary flicked forward to the *W*s again.

"And, just as I'm about to tell him, these two huge gates clang shut."

"Gates." Mary stopped flicking.

"And the wizard and the cat and the little house get smaller and smaller behind them until they disappear. And then I wake up feeling sad. That's about it really." Stella looked at Mary expectantly. "So what does all that mean?"

"You've had this dream how many times?"

"Three."

"And it's always the same?"

"Pretty much. I know that little house so well I think I could draw it. Hey, that's an idea! Would it help if I drew a picture for you?"

"No," Mary said. "It's all up here." She tapped her brow with the pencil. "You described it very well." She shut the Dream Decoder. "It's certainly a dream full of symbols. Too many symbols. Wands and wizards and cats and gates. They all mean something. It might take me some time. Payment in advance, please."

Stella gave her fifty cents.

"Sorry," Mary said. "I have to charge a dollar. This is a very complicated dream. But I'll give you the Express Service. You won't have to wait long."

Stella thought that sounded fair. She gave Mary another fifty cents.

The answer was passed to her during the last lesson of the day, hidden in the pages of a geography book. Stella removed the folded note and read what Mary had written:

Dreaming of food means you're hungry. Dreaming of gingerbread and candies and chocolate cookies means there is not enough sweetness in your life. The man in white with the hat is not a wizard, he's a chef and he's trying to feed you

(you are the skinny cat). But he can't because the doors of the fridge keep closing. (Do you have a fridge with two doors?) Eat some chocolate or ice cream before bed and the dream will go away.

Mary Sparkel, Dream Expert

Yes, thought Stella, the fridge at home *did* have double doors and she probably *was* a bit skinny. That could be because the fridge very seldom had anything in it. Neither of her busy parents had much time for shopping or cooking. But it was a good idea to eat more chocolate and ice cream. Mary certainly knew all about dreams.

Stella folded the note and slipped it into her pocket. But as she made her way home that afternoon, something about her dream, and Mary's answer, niggled away in her mind like an itchy insect bite that was just out of reach.

chapter *2

Lucille Seaton stood gazing out of the huge picture window, a look of deep satisfaction on her face. "Who could ever get tired of looking at this million-dollar coastal view?" she asked.

Stella went on turning the pages of the newspaper. She had learnt that it was best to ignore such questions. They weren't really questions and there was nothing to gain by being honest. If she said, "Well, me for one. I can think of a zillion more interesting things to do than look at the view," her mother would get cross and say, "Stella, you don't

9

deserve to live in a stunning penthouse apartment in a prime seaside location."

Lucille Seaton was in real estate, which was why she said things like that. In fact, she was a Real Estate Agent. "Lucille's Listings"—descriptions and color pictures of expensive and desirable houses for sale—appeared three times a week in the city and suburban newspapers, with a glamorous photograph of Lucille heading each column. She did all her own radio ads (*Hello, homebuyers, this is Lucille with another luxurious listing . . .*), and every week she had her hair and nails done and went on morning television to chat about *immaculately presented lifestyle opportunities in prime locations.*

That was real-estate language for "a neat house for sale in a nice street." But nobody in real estate ever said anything so simple and honest. Stella had decoded the language long ago. (In her way, Stella was as clever at decoding real-estate language as Mary Sparkel was at decoding dreams.) For example, "renovator's delight" meant an old house that was falling down around you. "Natural aircondi-tioning" meant there would be cracks in the walls big enough to push your fist through and gaps under all the doors. If the doors had fallen off com-pletely, that was "open-plan living." Rats and mice living under the floorboards and possums in the ceiling? "An abundance of wildlife."

Lucille, however, rarely dealt in properties that were old and run-down, and most of them were too high up in the sky for any rats and mice. And high in the sky was exactly where the Seaton fam-ily now lived.

Lucille had personally sold more than half the apartments in the new and ultra-modern Bayview Tower, but not before she had snapped up the penthouse. "It's an exciting opportunity to live an enviable beachfront lifestyle," she told Stella enthusiastically. Two months ago, Stella and her parents had moved in.

Stella was less enthusiastic. She'd lived four different lifestyles in the last six years and she hadn't enjoyed any of them. First, they'd lived in a Japanese house with bamboo screens instead of walls, mats instead of chairs and beds, and a pebble courtyard instead of a backyard. That had been followed by an inner-city converted warehouse with no walls at all (instead of a bedroom, Stella had a "sleeping platform"); a houseboat moored permanently on the Port River (no garden, no pets, no neighbors), and a Balinese pavilion with temple bells and waterfalls (but no backyard).

Now here they were, high in the sky. Which was not exactly beachfront, in Stella's opinion. You couldn't even hear the sea unless you opened the sliding doors. And when you did, the wind swept through the living room like a mini-cyclone and set the white silk curtains flapping like distress flags. Lucille would call out, "Stella, close those doors! It interferes with the airconditioning."

Nor could you walk out the front door and smell the sea and wiggle your toes in the sand. First you had to:

- Go out the door of the apartment and press the button for the elevator
- Wait for the elevator to come
- Use your electronic card then whizz down to the marble foyer
- Use your card again to open the electronic entrance doors
- Walk through the ginkgo garden and the Japanese shoji gates
- Walk along the sidewalk
- Cross the grass past the sidewalk

- Press the button at the pedestrian crossing and wait for the green light
- Cross the Esplanade
- Walk past the new marina
- Enter the shopping arcade
- Walk past a lot of shops and restaurants
- Exit the arcade and go onto the Promenade
- Walk down the steps to the beach

Coming home, of course, you had to do it all in reverse. It turned a simple walk on the beach into a major expedition. Most times, Stella couldn't be bothered.

Stella didn't like to complain. She knew there were plenty of people who would love to live in an open-plan penthouse with stunning ocean views. But she wasn't one of them. She would prefer to live in a normal house with a backyard big enough to throw a ball and for a dog to run around in.

Ah, a dog. That was another thing. Stella and her mother had The Dog Conversation approximately once a week. (Stella: "Please, Mom, can I have a dog?" Lucille: "For the hundredth time, Stella, no.") A penthouse apartment, her mother said firmly, was No Place For a Dog. In fact, it would be downright *cruel* to keep an active animal confined within four walls, even if they did encompass two hundred square yards of luxury living.

"Dogs need regular exercise, Stella. They need lots of space and dirt to dig in. They leave hair on the rugs and upholstery. They leave little messes everywhere. And dogs bark. The neighbors will complain. A dog wouldn't be happy here, darling."

Translation: "*I* wouldn't be happy with a dog." And what neighbors? Stella wondered.

In two months she'd hardly met anyone, apart from fellow travellers in the elevator. Sometimes they smiled and said hello; sometimes they ignored her completely. Stella knew she must have neighbors because their cars filled the underground parking garage and their windows shone brightly at night. But Bayside Tower was no vertical version of a TV show, where people flitted in and out of each other's lives and kitchens, and exchanged friendly gossip over the back fence.

And that was another thing. Even if by some chance they did move to a house on the ground with a big backyard in which a dog could play and dig, Stella knew it wouldn't stay like that for long. That was because her father, Henry, was an expert at turning ordinary backyards into extraordinary gardens. He was so good he had his own TV show. People would be sent away for the weekend while Henry and his team secretly got to work. The people would come back to find their boring old backyard transformed with crazy paving, pebble paths, water features, decorative rocks, timber decks, tropical ferns, fountains, birdbaths, Mexican mosaics, Thai temples or Tuscan urns. Invariably, they screamed with joy, which Stella could never understand. The old backyards always looked so much more comfortable and homely.

"This is certainly a prestige property," Lucille said, drawing the silk curtains and closing off the million-dollar view. "Perfectly designed for relaxed living." She looked around the huge living room and frowned. "Stella, don't leave the paper strewn across the sofa. You know the newsprint leaves smudges on the white leather. And I've told you a hundred times to take your school shoes off at the door and not to eat and drink in the living room. I don't want anything spilt on this carpet."

Stella gathered up the newspaper. What a dumb idea to lay cream carpet in a beachside apartment, she thought. It was bound to show every mark and every grain of sand.

In the kitchen, which gleamed with stainless-steel state-of-the-art equipment (very little of it used), Stella spread the newspaper over the granite top of the breakfast bar and took up her scissors. Every Thursday, Saturday and Sunday it was her job to clip the "Lucille's Listings" from the newspapers and paste them into a large scrap-book. For this, her mother paid her five dollars a week. She also clipped interesting articles about gardens for Henry, who paid her fifty cents for each one. As the papers were always full of gardening stories, Stella's finances were in a very healthy state.

As usual, there was not a single residence Stella felt the slightest desire to live in. *Can you imagine living like a movie star in this magnificent apartment with its split-level ambience and multiple garaging?*

No, Stella couldn't.

She turned the page. Her attention was caught by a small advertisement tucked away at the bottom of the last page:

For Sale: **Playhouse**
16 Florence Street, Bayside.
Solid timber with balcony and ladder.
Run-down, neglected; needs work and TLC.
$150 neg. 555-7663

---

chapter ✿ 3

Stella's first thought was that it was a funny place to advertise a playhouse, right in the middle of advertisements for Executive Living and Country Properties.

Her second thought was that the address must be very near Bayview Tower.

Her third thought was that the owner didn't know much about real-estate language. It should say something like "Handyman's dream, ripe for renovation." And what was TLC?

She asked her mother, who was down on her

hands and knees picking fluff out of the cream pile of the living-room carpet.

"Tender loving care," Lucille said. "Why?"

"There's a house for sale that needs it."

"That usually means it's a complete dump," Lucille said.

Stella read the advertisement again. Something tugged at her heart. A little house that had been neglected. (Had its children grown up and left home?) A little wooden house with a ladder and a balcony. A little house that needed tender loving care.

Then something tugged at her mind. Her dream. The question that the wizard had asked her. The question she hadn't answered in the dream. The question that Mary Sparkel should have asked her.

Stella, what do you want most in the world?

In the dream she didn't ever have an opportunity to answer. Just as she'd open her mouth to

reply, the big gates would clang shut and everything would disappear. And, funnily enough, she
never gave much thought to the question when
she woke up. It was, after all, a Big Question,
one quite different from, "What would you buy if
somebody sent you fifty dollars?"

Now she knew the answer.

What she wanted most in the world was a place
of her own. She would have been satisfied with a
room with four solid walls and a door she could
shut and which she could decorate to suit herself.
But a little wooden house with a balcony! She was
too old for one of those baby playhouses, but this
sounded perfect.

Where could she put it, though? Not in the
apartment, despite its open plan and heaps of
space. For one thing, it would leave a mark on the
cream carpet. Not on the wide balconies; they were
already crammed with potted trees and designer

patio pieces, as Lucille called the chairs and recliner sofas. Not in the underground parking garage—too gloomy. Not in the Japanese ginkgo garden—too public.

Her mother bustled into the kitchen. "Darling, call Daddy and ask him to bring home something from Tasty Take-out, will you? I haven't had time to shop and now I have to work on my new sales campaign. Are these today's clippings? Good." Grabbing them, she bustled out again.

Stella considered the price of the playhouse— *$150 neg. Neg* meant negotiable: the owner might take a lower price. She had $91.50 in her savings account and $7.85 in her piggy bank. That was just under a hundred dollars. Would the seller go that low? Probably not.

Two problems then: price and location. How could she pay for it? Where could she put it? No solution came to mind. But didn't she have a Real

Estate Agent on hand? She climbed the spiral stair-case that led to the mezzanine, where her mother had her office workspace.

"What would you do," Stella asked, "if there was this cool house you really really wanted but you didn't have enough money to buy it and you didn't have a lot of land to put it on?"

"As an investment or to live in?" Lucille asked, not looking away from her computer screen.

"To live in."

"Is a housing loan out of the question?"

Stella considered. "I think so. Yes."

"I'd rent," Lucille said. "Of course, it's always better to be paying off your own home rather than lining a landlord's pocket, but sometimes renting is an acceptable short-term solution."

Of course! Why hadn't she thought of that? "Thanks, Mom." Stella clattered back down the staircase.

"Have you called your father yet?"

"I'll do it now."

"Thai, I think. Perhaps a green curry. Depends on what Daddy had for lunch. Call him on his cell phone and ask."

Stella's mind was buzzing with her brilliant idea. She didn't want to waste time discussing the menu items of the Tasty Take-out with her father. She picked up her mother's cell phone which was lying on the kitchen counter and sent him a text message instead: *Pls get tie from TT c u l8r*. Then she remembered Mary Sparkel's advice and added, *+ ice cream*.

She picked up the scissors and carefully clipped out the advertisement for the playhouse. Where exactly was Florence Street?

If there was one thing the Seaton family had plenty of, it was street directories. Lucille had one in her car and Henry had one in his. There was another in Lucille's mezzanine office and another near the wall phone in the kitchen. Stella flipped it open and noted the map grids. She found the right page and yes, there was Florence Street, at the southern end of the Esplanade and not more than a thumb's width from Bayview Tower. She could go there tomorrow, after school.

Should she call first? Well, there was really no question about that. Hadn't she heard her mother say over and over that the two most important factors in real estate were location and timing? The advertisement didn't mention any open inspections but, right at this minute, eager playhouse buyers could be calling Florence Street and making negotiable offers, sight unseen. It might already have been sold.

Feeling quite jittery with excitement and nerves, Stella punched in the number. It rang for so long she began to worry that she was too late and the house had already been sold. Obviously nobody was sitting waiting for offers. But then someone picked up the phone and a man's gruff voice said, "Hello."

"Um, I'm calling about the playhouse," Stella said.

"The what?"

"The playhouse. The one for sale in this morning's paper. Is this the right number?"

"Oh, the playhouse. My mind was elsewhere."

Stella brightened. Obviously the phone hadn't been ringing off the hook all day with prospective buyers. "So you haven't sold it yet?"

"No, it's still here. A few people said they'd come and see it on Saturday. Maybe they will, maybe they won't."

Tomorrow was Friday. "I can come tomorrow," Stella said.

"It'll probably still be here."

Now what? Stella wondered. It might be a good idea to demonstrate some serious interest by asking a few questions, the sort that people asked her mother.

"Does it have a flexible flooring plan?"

"A what?"

"Um, how many rooms and walls and things?"

"Four walls, one room. You were expecting more?"

He sounded a bit grumpy, Stella thought. "Does it have a high ceiling? What about window treatments and rear access?"

"What exactly are you looking for, young lady? This is a playhouse, not a townhouse." Now he sounded cross.

"Sorry, I'm a bit nervous," she said. "I've wanted a playhouse for a long time." Which was quite true, even if she hadn't actually realized it until now.

"Well, you'd better come and see it then."

"I can't come until after school. Would four

o'clock be okay?"

"I'll be here. I usually am."

"You won't sell it before I get there, will you?"

"Can't give a guarantee. Someone might come in the morning and offer me my price right away. I'd be silly to say no, wouldn't I?"

Stella sighed. "I guess so. There's no place for sentiment when it comes to selling a house." How often had she heard her mother say that?

There was a little explosion on the end of the line, as if the man had laughed and sneezed at the same time. "You going to tell me your name?"

"Stella. Stella Seaton."

This time he really did laugh. "Well, you certainly got the right name," he said. "See you tomorrow."

What did he mean by that? Stella wondered, putting down the phone. Then she understood. He'd made the connection with Lucille Seaton

Real Estate.

The front door of the apartment opened and her father appeared.

"I'm home! What's for dinner?"

He wasn't carrying any Tasty Take-out bags.

Her mother's head appeared over the mezzanine railing. "Henry? You were supposed to pick up dinner. Didn't Stella call you?"

"Dinner? I got a text message about picking up a tie from TT, whoever he is. Don't need any more ties so I didn't bother. Got the ice cream though. Actually, I left it in the car. Stell, go and get it, will you?" He threw her the car keys.

"Stella!"

Ignoring her mother, Stella made her escape. At least she had her ice cream. No wizard dreams tonight!

chapter ✿ 4

Florence Street was not at all easy to find. Some of it had been gobbled up by the recent high-rise developments—of which Bayview Tower was one—that spread along and out from the Esplanade. Consequently, the street didn't start where the atlas (clearly outdated, Stella now realized) said it did, and there was no logic to the house numbers. It was a good thing, Stella thought, shifting her backpack to a more comfortable position, that she'd spent so many weekends driving around the city with her mother looking for properties.

She trudged past a row of new Mediterranean townhouses with their locked gates and intercoms and then stopped. She was definitely at the end of Florence Street. Ahead of her was the Esplanade, a block of high-rise apartments on the left corner, the gentle rise of the sandhills (or what was left of them) on her right. Beyond the Esplanade was the dazzling blue of the sea. But no other properties. So number sixteen had to be one of the Mediter-ranean townhouses. Stella was surprised. They didn't look like the sort of places that would have a wooden playhouse in the backyard. Actually, they didn't look as if they would have backyards at all. These were definitely what her mother called courtyard homes.

She was about to retrace her steps when she noticed something she'd missed: a narrow unpaved pathway running along the side of the townhouses and, at the end of it, the tip of a red iron roof through a clump of green foliage.

Aha! Stella made her way down the pathway. She could guess what had happened. Number sixteen, which must originally have been a large corner property, had sold its Florence Street frontage to the developers. Now it was tucked away at the rear of the townhouses. And tucked away at its own rear was, Stella hoped, her playhouse. Well, not hers yet, but if her offer was accepted, wouldn't it be funny to put a little birdhouse behind it? Then there'd be a house behind the townhouses and a playhouse behind the house and a birdhouse behind the playhouse . . .

She stopped as the house came into view, her mouth opening in surprise. Oh, Mary Sparkel, she thought, I wish you could see this!

In the late-afternoon sunshine, the old stone walls of the house glowed golden-brown. Stella stared at the gabled roofline, the return veranda with lacy wooden fretwork like icing on a wedding cake and turned posts like candy canes. The windows were trimmed in white and above the dark timber door glowed a fan of colorful track lighting. It looked, Stella thought, rather like a chocolate cookie topped with shiny red and green sprinkles.

Almost unable to breathe, she walked towards it along a path edged with rose bushes. Not ripe raspberries, she realized: red roses. And weren't those fir trees in the front of the house exactly the shape of spearmint leaves? Goodness me, Stella thought, any minute now a wizard and a black cat are going to appear . . .

Meooow!

Stella jumped. She hadn't noticed it but, curled up on the edge of the veranda like a dozing sentinel, the cat had noticed her. It stood up, arched its back, and came to inspect her.

By now, Stella was feeling more than a little bit

nervous. Despite the jolly appearance of the story-book house, it *was* rather isolated, tucked away from the street and behind the sandhills. (And why hadn't she remembered the story of Hansel and Gretel?) If anything nasty happened, would anybody in the townhouses hear her cries for help? Stella doubted it. If she knocked on that chocolate-cookie door and it was opened by an old wizard with long white hair and a pointed hat ... Nevermind the playhouse, she was going to turn and run!

Meoow! The cat rubbed against her leg and purred. Well, at least one of the occupants was friendly. Stella squatted to stroke it and thus was in a perfect position to take in the pair of tall black boots which, right at that moment, came clomping round the corner of the house. Dangling above them, a gloved hand clutched a wicked blade.

Stella's heart lurched and her mouth went dry.

The black boots stopped.

"And who have we got here?" a gruff voice said.

Stella's frightened eyes remained fixed on the boots. *Rubber* boots. She raised her eyes a little. Faded blue jeans, mud-stained. And not a blade, but pruning shears. She gave a little sigh of relief and got rather shakily to her feet.

Right at her eye level was a large silver star. And further up, silhouetted against the sky, a big pointed hat.

Stella gulped. "Oh, Mary Sparkel!" she whispered.

"Mary who?" said the wizard. "I was expecting a Stella."

"That's me," Stella said.

"That's what I thought. You found the house all right, then? Some people never find it."

"I'm used to finding houses," Stella said. Now that she'd shaded her eyes and the man had advanced a few paces, she could see that he wasn't really a wizard. Well, not unless wizards wore black sweatshirts that said "Lone Star Beer" and straw hats.

The man saw her staring at it. "Like my hat?" He took it off and Stella saw that he had long white hair caught in a rubber band at the nape of his neck. "Best thing for gardening, keeps the sun off, doesn't make you sweat, never needs washing." He pulled off his gardening gloves and threw them into the hat. "I suppose you want to see the playhouse?"

"Yes, please," Stella said. She didn't feel nervous at all now. Wizards might do the odd bit of gardening (pumpkins for Halloween? herbs for magic potions?) but she was sure they didn't sweat or concern themselves with laundry.

"It's round the back. Follow me."

The black cat came too. "What's your cat's name?" Stella asked.

"Wouldn't have a clue. Not my cat. Belongs to

one of them." He waved in the direction of the townhouses. "She seems to like sleeping on my veranda. I call her Blackie."

Not very imaginative, Stella thought, but again she felt reassured. A wizard's cat would be called Hepzibah or Mephistopheles, not Blackie.

At the rear of the house was an enormous backyard. Except for its size, it resembled the sort of yard that Stella had seen a hundred times before: a strip of cracked concrete bordered a large overgrown grassy area (it couldn't really be called a lawn) studded with fruit trees and edged with straggly shrubs. A few dish towels flapped from a sagging clothesline. There was a brick barbecue leaning against the side of a rather dilapidated garage; a simple wooden table and benches under a vine-covered trellis; an old black bike propped up against a water tank on a wooden stand. It was a wonderful backyard, the kind Henry and his team would completely demolish and transform in forty-eight hours.

But no playhouse.

The man, however, hadn't stopped, and now Stella could see that the yard didn't end at the edge of the grass but continued past a green hedge, which turned out not to be hedge at all but frames of climbing beans and tomatoes, and next to them beds of leafy vegetables. And right at the back and at the end of a gravel path, high up on wooden posts like stilts, was the timber playhouse.

"That's the side view. You know why it's not facing this way?"

Stella shook her head.

"Come and see."

She followed him round to the front of the playhouse and now she could see the ladder with its steps leading up to the balcony, made secure by a wooden railing and a cross-bar. There was a front door and a window with wooden shutters. The roof was pitched with a little weathervane atop the gable and a downpipe which led from the gutters to a silver water tank situated underneath the balcony.

Stella gazed at it in delight.

chapter ✳ 5

"Well, go on," the man said. He gestured with his head towards the ladder. "Look out for the third step, it's a bit wobbly."

Stella put down her backpack and climbed up while he stood below and watched. He really wasn't very experienced at this sort of thing, she noted. Lucille would never draw attention to a fault. Nor would she allow potential buyers to wander around unaccompanied. "They miss things, Stella. You have to point out features like built-ins and original fireplaces and under-floor heating. Some people would miss the view if you didn't show it to them."

The view? Stella went to the railing and gazed out over the balcony.

"Not bad, eh?" the man called.

Stella grinned. She could just imagine her mother standing in front of this uninterrupted view across the sandhills to the long stretch of golden beach and white-capped blue sea and saying to her potential buyer, "Not bad, eh?" But what else did you really need to say when it was there spread before you, filling your eyes and your ears and your nostrils? She sniffed the fresh salty air appreciatively. You could almost taste the beach when you were this close.

"Not bad," she agreed. The railing, she noticed, wasn't as firmly anchored as it might have been.

"You'll want to inspect the flexible flooring plan. I'll leave you to it. Come in the back door when you're through."

He stumped off down the path, the black cat following at his heels. Stella appreciated the chance to be alone and she had no intention of missing anything. She turned and pushed open the front door, noting as she did so its tendency to stick but observing at the same time that it was a very nice front door, with a carved knob like a flower and a starburst of green and blue glass in the top panel.

It was just one room, of course, but there were several features, like the overhead lights, that set it apart from your run-of-the-mill playhouses. It had electricity, for one thing. A bare bulb, which hung from the center of the ceiling, lit up when Stella flicked the switch by the front door, and another light went on over the balcony. There was a window seat, almost wide enough to be a narrow bed, whose top flipped open to reveal a generous storage bin. Her mother would certainly have pointed that out. "You can never have enough built-ins, Stella." There was a wooden table and two chairs, one of them broken, and Stella wondered whether they were included in the price. They couldn't be called fixtures or fittings. But the shelves could, because they were attached to the walls, and so could the twin cupboards on the far wall. That's where I'll store my dishes and food, Stella thought. She opened one of the doors and it promptly fell off its hinges. The inside of the cupboard was dusty, too. In fact, the whole playhouse needed a good wash and sweep. Not to mention a few nails in strategic places.

Stella took a notebook and pen from her backpack and went around the interior, listing all the things that needed attention. Then she went outside and did the same. When she finished, it was quite a long list. The owner had certainly been honest: the playhouse was neglected; it did need a lot of TLC. But at $150 it was still a bargain. Lucille could have got him twice the price.

But none of this mattered to Stella. Oh, how she wanted this little house! It was made for her. She could picture herself stocking the pantry cupboard, collecting dishes and glasses, decorating the bare walls with colorful prints and posters, sitting on the balcony reading a book and smelling the sea air, tramping across the sandhills for a swim and hanging her wet towel on the railing, inviting Jade and Mary over for lunch . . .

First, though, she had some negotiating to do. She closed the front door and went carefully down the ladder, watching out for the wobbly step. She walked slowly along the path, rehearsing various openings in her mind. "Never admit how much you want a property," her mother would say. "Begin with all the things that are wrong with it, and then start bargaining."

She tapped on the back screen door.

"Come on through!"

The warm smell of baking made her nostrils twitch appreciatively the minute she walked in. Stella was suddenly very hungry indeed. She looked around the old-fashioned kitchen with its linoleum floor, scrubbed pine table piled with vegetables, ancient gas stove and the sink under the window crowded with dirty dishes, and thought it was one of the nicest kitchens she'd ever seen. Her mother would say that was because of the smell: it was an old real-estate trick to have bread in the oven or coffee on the stove during an open inspection. "It creates a homey ambience, Stella."

"Have a seat," the man said. He'd taken off his gardening gloves and rubber boots and was wearing a pair of brown-checked slippers. "Want a sticky bun?" He put a plate on the table in front of her.

Stella took one. It was warm from the oven, the

sugar glaze slightly moist. She bit into it. It was delicious.

The man sat down opposite her and also took a bun. "Well, what's the verdict?"

"It's excellent," Stella said. "The shop ones never have enough pecans."

"I was referring to the playhouse. But thank you for the compliment."

"The playhouse is excellent, too," Stella said. And then, all in a rush, forgetting her bargaining plan entirely, she said, "It's a beautiful playhouse and I really really want it, you can't guess how much, it's exactly right for me, I even had a dream about you and this house and I'm so glad you haven't sold it yet, would you take an offer?"

The man continued chewing on his mouthful of bun. "Needs a bit of work," he said. "There's that third step, and I suppose you noticed the door sticks."

"Not so very much."

"The cupboard door's off its hinges."

"A few screws will fix that."

"There's a couple of loose floorboards and the balcony railing needs support. A few nails in the roof wouldn't hurt either, might even have to replace the iron."

"I like the water tank," Stella said. "Not many playhouses have their own fresh water supply."

"The gutters are probably clogged. Need a good clean and scrub. The whole house needs a good scrub, come to think of it."

"Does the furniture come with it?"

He waved his hand dismissively. "That old table and broken chairs? I'd have to pay someone to take them away."

"They're absolutely fine," Stella said. "And so is the playhouse. It just needs a little TLC like your advertisement said. Did you build it for your children?"

"Years ago. They live out of state now. I don't see much of them. Wasn't much point keeping the playhouse. I have enough to do keeping this old place shipshape without looking after that one too."

"It's certainly worth $150," Stella said. "Probably more."

"I can see you're going to be a tough bargainer," the man said. "Have another sticky bun, it looks like we're in for a long session. What's your offer?"

"Well." Here was the tricky bit. Stella opened her backpack and took out a manila file and a calculator. She put it next to her notebook and pen. "Your asking price is $150—"

"Negotiable."

Stella nodded. "And it's certainly worth that. The thing is, though, I haven't got quite that amount." She opened the notebook and checked her figures, even though the numbers were engraved on her brain. "I have ninety-nine dollars and thirty-five cents. Let's say one hundred dollars." She could probably find sixty-five cents in coins stuck down the back of the sofa or on the floor of her mother's car or even in the washing machine.

"That's your offer? For a solid timber playhouse with a balcony and a water tank?"

"I know it's worth more and you should wait because probably lots of people will come on the weekend to inspect it and when they do you won't have any problem getting your asking price because it's such a superior playhouse but—"

"I accept your offer. Ninety-nine dollars and thirty-five cents. Forget about the small change, make it ninety-nine dollars." He stood up. "All that bargaining has worn me out. How about a cup of tea?"

Stella gaped at him. "You'll accept that price?"

"I said it was negotiable, didn't I? Well, we've

negotiated. You're satisfied, I'm satisfied." He turned from filling the kettle at the sink and looked at her. "Aren't you?"

"There's a bit more to my offer," Stella said, still in shock. My goodness, who could have predicted this turn of events? A vendor who accepted a ridiculously low price and then offered her a discount! He didn't know how the real-estate game worked at all. If only she had a backyard!

"The thing is," Stella said, "I don't have a backyard. I live at the top of Bayview Tower. There's nowhere to put a playhouse, especially one with a balcony and a water tank. So what I was hoping for was a sort of rental arrangement."

"Rental?"

The man looked puzzled. Stella reminded herself that he didn't know much about real estate. She opened her file. "It could work like this. I'd pay you rent in advance, four weeks is usual, plus a security deposit. That's in case I break something—but I wouldn't, I'd be very careful—or leave suddenly without paying my rent, but I wouldn't do that either. So it just depends on what you think a fair rent would be. We could sign a contract and make it all legal, and if you want a reference I could get one from my teacher—"

The man held up his hand. "Hold your horses. I want to *sell* the playhouse, get rid of it. I don't want someone *living* in it at the bottom of my yard."

"I wouldn't exactly be living there," Stella pointed out. "I mean, I do have parents and a bedroom, and I have to go to school five days a week, so I'd hardly be there at all really, just after school and on weekends. And I'm very quiet. I don't have lots of friends and I wouldn't have loud parties and I don't have any pets." This, she knew, was strongly in her favor. Landlords didn't like noisy tenants with active social lives.

"Why not?"

"Why not what?" Stella asked, frowning.

"Why don't you have many friends?"

"We haven't lived here long, so I'm new at school." Stella explained about the Japanese house and the converted warehouse and the Balinese pavilion and the houseboat on the river. "We're always moving so it's hard to make friends. And there's really nowhere to play at home."

"Hard to keep pets too, I guess."

Stella nodded sadly. "I've never had a pet."

"I dare say Blackie would come and visit you, especially if you put a saucer of milk out on the balcony."

Stella looked at him hopefully. "You'd be willing to rent me the playhouse?"

"A tenant in the backyard wasn't exactly what I had in mind. But as long as you're quiet and don't get in my hair, I guess we could see how it works out. Don't expect me to fix things or clean the place up. I'm not that sort of landlord. What sort of rental were you thinking of?"

Stella checked her notebook again. She'd calculated the figure, based on her average weekly earnings over the past two months and remembering her mother's advice that rent should never be more than fifty percent of your income. "Would $6.50 a week be fair?" she asked. "I wouldn't use much electricity because I wouldn't be here at night."

The man shook his head. "You drive a hard bargain, young lady, but you sound like an ideal tenant. Let's say five dollars a week."

Stella felt a rush of happiness. "I brought along a contract," she said, opening the file and taking it out. "Just in case."

He waved it aside. "Too complicated. We can write our own. May I borrow your pen?" He scribbled a few lines on the back—very few, Stella noted—and handed it to her. "Sign at the bottom if that suits."

Stella read: "The landlord of playhouse number 16a, Florence Street, Bayside, agrees to rent the property to the tenant for five dollars a week. The contract can be terminated at any time by mutual agreement and with one week's notice."

"You forgot about the deposit and rent in advance," she said.

"You look trustworthy. I don't think that'll be necessary."

"I'm very trustworthy," Stella assured him. She took the pen and signed her name next to the word "Tenant." She pushed it across the table and watched as the man scribbled his name next to "Landlord." Stella looked at it: she ought to know the name of her brand new landlord. But he had very scribbly writing. "Charles?" she said.

"Chester."

"Sorry, Chester . . . Wizard?" she squeaked.

"Vizard. V-i-z-a-r-d." He pronounced it *Vyezard*. "You can call me Chester if you like. So, Stella Seaton. I said you had the right name."

"The right name?" Stella was still feeling dazed. "You mean for real estate?"

"This real estate anyway. Stella means 'star,' doesn't it?"

"Does it?"

"Certainly. From the Latin. Didn't you notice the colored star above the playhouse door? And the nameplate? No, that fell off a long time ago. I'll have to put it back up. Anyway, that's the playhouse's name: *Stella Maris*, Star of the Sea. And you're a Stella Seaton. Seaton means 'the town or dwellings by the sea,' so practically the same thing."

Stella was amazed. "I told you I had a dream about all this. There was a star in it too."

"It was obviously meant to be. Names and

dreams can be very prophetic. Now, how do you like your tea?"

They drank tea and ate the rest of the sticky buns and talked about when Stella might move in some of her belongings, and then Chester walked her down to the front gate. A wad of junk mail was sticking out from his mailbox. "Supermarkets and real-estate agents!" he growled. "Wasting trees and cluttering up the mail. This one's the worst." He crumpled a flyer in his hand, but not before Stella had recognized the distinctive pink lettering of Lucille Seaton Real Estate. "She's always calling and writing and pestering me to sell."

Stella could feel her cheeks flushing as pink as the flyer. How could she confess Lucille was her mother? Chester might give her a week's notice. "I suppose that's because you're in a prime location," she said. "And haven't you already sold some of your front yard?" She pointed to the townhouses.

"Yes," said Chester, looking as though he regretted it. "I gave the money to my children so they could buy their own places."

"The ones who live out of state?" Stella asked, and Chester nodded. It occurred to her that he might want to join them. "You're not thinking of selling your house, are you?" she asked anxiously.

Chester shook his head. "No, I'm too old to move and I like living here by the sea, so I don't suppose I'll ever sell." He grinned. "Well, not unless I'm offered a million dollars."

chapter * 6

For the next few weeks, Stella's head was filled with thoughts of her new home. Every minute spent away from it was a minute wasted, in her opinion. She lay in bed at night running over in her mind the repairs still to be done (not many, because Chester had fixed the door and the wobbly step and the cupboard even before she had moved in) and the bits and pieces she needed (a rug for the floor, a deck chair for the balcony). At school, when she was supposed to be dissecting a seed pod or writing about the importance of the water buffalo in Indonesia, she found herself sketching little home improvements, like a padded top for the window seat, a garden patch and some potted plants, and perhaps a clothesline. Her mother was right: towels draped over the balcony was not a good look.

She started reading the glossy magazines her mother brought home and it was surprising, given that most of the houses in them were fifty times bigger and about a squillion dollars more expensive, how often she found something she could adapt for *Stella Maris*. (Chester had found the nameplate and screwed it on the wall next to the front door.) An old batik sarong Lucille had thrown out looked very attractive draped around the playhouse's window, and a copper mixing bowl made a striking light fitting. Her mother never even noticed its absence. Why would she? As far as Stella could remember, nobody in the family had ever cooked anything that called for a copper mixing bowl.

Her parents did, however, notice her frequent absences. Stella had pondered long and hard on how much she should reveal about her new status as a tenant. On the one hand, they had a right to know where she was disappearing to on weekends. (After school wasn't a problem: as long as she was back in the penthouse by six o'clock, nobody was home early enough to notice her absence.) On the other hand, she didn't want either of them interfering. She knew the moment she said, "Oh, by the way, I've signed a lease on a playhouse by the sea, just behind the sandhills on the south Esplanade, and I'll be spending a lot of my free time there from now on," she would never have it to herself again. Lucille would swish around with her color charts and wallpaper samples and fabric swathes, rearranging and rehanging and refurbishing, and effecting what she called "stunning statements." Henry would landscape to within an inch of the sandhills, and instead of grass and sand she'd have pebble paving, a water feature and a gazebo. No, she had to keep them both away from *Stella Maris*.

In the end she just said casually, in answer to her mother's inquiry, "Oh, didn't I tell you? I've got a new friend who lives just along the Esplanade. There's a big backyard and it's really close to the beach."

Her mother was so pleased to hear she had a friend that instead of saying pointedly, "We're near the beach too, Stella," she just smiled and said, "That's nice, dear. What's your friend's name?"

Stella considered. If she said Chester, her mother might say, "A boy? You're spending all this time alone with a boy? I don't much like the sound of *that*." At least, it was what Stella assumed her mother would say. She'd never had a boyfriend so she couldn't be sure. It was what Jade's mother said whenever Jade announced, as she did every Saturday afternoon, that she was going over to Cody Palmer's house to watch videos. On the other hand, she didn't want to lie. So she said, "Chessie."

"Chessie? That's a sweet name. Is it a new house?" As usual, her mother was more interested in the real estate than the person.

"No, an old one."

"Does it have a beach frontage?"

"No," said Stella. Well, the playhouse did, but number sixteen fronted the Mediterranean townhouses.

"A pity. Seafront properties are bringing *huge* prices now." Her mother lost interest and Stella was safe.

Stella quickly fell into a routine. After school and

every weekend, as soon as her parents had left the house (Saturdays and Sundays were Henry and Lucille's busiest days), she would go straight to Florence Street. She'd collect her mail and Chester's too, if he hadn't done so already. "You're a tenant, you must have your own mailbox," he'd insisted a few days after Stella had signed the lease. And almost before she could blink, there it was, right next to his, marked 16a. Stella had protested (weakly, because she liked the idea of having her own mailbox) that it was quite unnecessary because she rarely got mail, but that depended, of course, on your definition of mail. Hardly a day went by when there wasn't something in her mailbox: catalogues, vouchers for fast food and videos, the occasional sample of a new detergent or cleaning product (very useful, these), letters from the local mayor addressed "To the Householder," which made Stella feel very important, and endless appeals from real-estate agents. (*Are you thinking of selling? We currently have a list of buyers looking for prestige properties in Bayside* . . .) These she dropped straight in the trash bin, along with the ones in Chester's mailbox. Many of the letters were from Lucille Seaton Real Estate and Stella felt a few pangs of guilt as she chucked the envelopes with the familiar pink logo on top of the molding vegetable scraps and discarded cans. But the last thing she wanted was for the new landlord to sell up.

After sorting through the mail, Stella would walk around the side of the house and across the grass and past the rows of beans and cabbages and then her playhouse would come into view with Blackie sunning herself on the balcony, and her heart would give a sort of happy little skip. Every single time. Her mother had often talked of something she called "pride of ownership" and finally Stella knew what it was.

In the early days, and mindful of Chester's grumbled instructions to stay out of his hair, Stella had been careful not to disturb him. But Chester didn't seem to mind being disturbed. In fact, Stella often had the feeling that he was actually listening out for her. No matter how quiet she was, he would hear her footsteps and emerge from the back door bearing a plate of freshly baked goodies. Chester, it turned out, was a retired pastry chef who had once worked in some of the great restaurants of Europe. He hadn't lost his touch, even though, as he told Stella, he'd pretty much put away his baking sheets and closed his oven door for good. "You were baking sticky buns the first day I came," Stella pointed out. "That's because I knew you were coming," Chester said. "There's no point in baking for one, is there?"

There was, apparently, a point in baking for two and part of the fun of arriving at *Stella Maris* was trying to guess what mouth-watering treats would be waiting for her: apple strudel, strawberry short-cake, chocolate eclairs, individual custard tarts topped with slices of glazed fruits, blueberry muffins, doughnuts dusted with sugar, flaky pies and cream-topped meringues . . .

Stella might well have ballooned into a little pork sausage on two legs if she hadn't met the neighbors and had her Bright Idea.

She hadn't quite given up her desire for a dog and was delighted when she found one, a small black labrador, under her balcony one Saturday. Only after they'd made friends and played on the beach had Stella looked at the medallion on his collar and discovered his name—Jules—and his address: one of the Mediterranean townhouses. When she'd seen signs that they were home later that afternoon she'd returned him and so met Jeffrey and Shane. Jeffrey worked as a florist and Shane was a hair stylist and neither of them had time to give Jules regular exercise. For a split second, Stella had been tempted to say what her mother would surely have said: "In that case, why have a dog, especially one that needs a lot of exercise and space to run around in?" But she'd seen how they really did love Jules, so instead she said eagerly, "If you like, I could take him for a run. I'm here practically every day."

"That would be *wonderful*!" exclaimed Jeffrey.

"Oh, *super*!" exclaimed Shane. "We'd pay you, of course."

In vain did Stella protest that she loved dogs and would do it for free. "It's best to keep arrangements professional," Jeffrey said. "I could give you flowers in exchange and Shane could style your hair but in the long run money is *neater*, don't you think?"

On reflection, Stella did, especially when a Cavalier spaniel and a poodle joined her dog-walking group and her payment increased threefold. The former belonged to Marcel and Melissa, a young couple who wore dark suits and carried briefcases and drove home each evening in matching grey Celicas. The poodle belonged to Mrs. Adey, who had a weak leg and wore support stockings. And next door to her lived Mr. Lee, who was studying in college and was Blackie's owner. Stella met him and discovered the cat's name was Mao.

"But he can be Blackie at your house," Mr. Lee said generously.

"Blackie's a boy?" Stella said in surprise.

Everybody was intrigued to learn that she was renting Mr. Vizard's playhouse.

"He doesn't seem the sort who'd have a play-house," said Melissa, and Stella explained about the grown-up children who now lived far away.

"We've never really talked to him," said Shane. "He looks so grumpy."

"He's not grumpy at all," said Stella, forgetting that she'd once thought that herself. She described all the work Chester had done on the playhouse and how he gave her garden vegetables to take home and how he was teaching her to cook.

"He shouldn't be living alone in that big house,"Mrs. Adey said. "What if something happened to him?"

This *did* give Stella pause. Old people were always having accidents, she knew that. They fell down and broke their hips or they had heart attacks and if they lived alone they were found days later, either dead in bed or collapsed on the bathroom floor. What if Chester had an accident one night after she'd left Florence Street? He'd have to lie in agony for almost twenty-four hours before she returned.

What Chester needed, Stella realized, were neighbors. Not faceless, nameless neighbors like hers in Bayview Tower, but people who knew and looked out for each other and would notice immediately if anything was wrong. Not that she could tell Chester that. Chester liked to think he was independent. He certainly wasn't sociable: he'd made no attempt, after all, to get to know his town-house neighbors. So how could she bring everyone together without letting Chester know she was worried about him?

It was Jeffrey who gave her the answer. "I hope you're going to have a house-warming party," he said. "Shane and Jules and I love parties. You *will* invite us, won't you?"

"Of course I will," said Stella. "That's a brilliant idea. I'll have it next Sunday afternoon. But what will I do about food? There's no kitchen in the playhouse and I haven't got much money."

Jeffrey waved his hand as if it wasn't a problem at all. "Just tell everyone to bring a plate."

This, Stella discovered, didn't actually mean bring a plate, it meant bring a plate *of food*. All she had to do was to provide the drinks and borrow some plates and glasses from Chester. At first, he hadn't shown much enthusiasm for the party. "A lot of strangers clumping through the garden," he grumbled.

"They're not strangers," Stella said. "At least, they won't be afterwards. Don't you want to meet Jules's owners? And Melissa and Marcel and Mrs. Adey and Mr. Lee, who owns Blackie? They want to meet you."

"Can't think what for." But he'd given her the crockery and on Sunday morning he swept the garden path and at three o'clock he was the first to arrive with a huge tray of meringues and tarts and chocolate eclairs.

It was a wonderful party. Melissa and Marcel brought their CD player and Jeffrey taught everyone to tango. Then Mrs. Adey, despite her weak leg, showed them how to do a dance called the cha-cha. Shane put on his favorite song and led them around the balcony and up and down the stairs in the "Locomotion." Then Mr. Lee boiled the kettle and made jasmine tea and everybody scoffed down Chester's pastries and agreed they were simply *scrumptious*.

"It's nice to have neighbors, isn't it?" Stella asked, as she and Chester stood on the steps of the playhouse, waving everybody goodbye.

"As long as they're the right sort of neighbors," Chester said.

But clearly they were, because after that it was never a question of baking for one (or even two), and soon everybody in the Mediterranean townhouses was getting regular deliveries of strudel and cheesecakes or whatever Chester was baking that day. In exchange, Shane trimmed Chester's hair every month and Mr. Lee mowed his grass and Marcel bought him a beer or three and Mrs. Adey cooked him casseroles.

"They never leave a man alone," Chester grumbled to Stella. "As for baking, I'm at it all day long. Might as well be back at work."

By now Stella knew that what Chester said was often at odds with what Chester did, and that nothing gave him more pleasure than to see people enjoying his pastries. Which is why one day, about two months after she'd moved into *Stella Maris*, she invited Mary Sparkel to afternoon tea.

"Mary Sparkel?" he frowned. "Where have I heard that name before?" Then his brow cleared. "The day I met you, when you came to look at the playhouse. The girl who decoded your dream, right?"

Stella nodded. "Except she got it all wrong. She

said the gingerbread house meant there wasn't enough sweetness in my life and you weren't a wizard, you were a chef who was trying to feed me and—" She stopped abruptly. "Oh, my goodness!" she whispered.

"Quite a talent," Chester said. "I'm looking forward to meeting her. I've had some odd dreams myself lately. Here, have one of these croissants, they're just out of the oven."

chapter *7

"So you see," said Stella, "everything really did turn out pretty much how you said."

Mary Sparkel cut herself a large slice of lemon coconut sponge cake. "Naturally," she said. "I'm very rarely wrong on the important details."

"Well, you were a *little* off-beam," Stella said, slightly miffed at Mary's complete lack of humility and the fact that this was her third slice of cake (not to mention the two strawberry tarts and the chocolate pecan slice that had preceded it).

Mary raised an eyebrow. "Off-beam?"

"The gates. Remember how in my dream they closed and the wizard and the house and everything disappeared? You said they were fridge doors closing, but that can't be right. And I've got what I wanted most in the world."

"Gates or doors, it's all the same. If they close it's bad news."

Stella stared at her. "You mean all this—" she looked around her glorious little playhouse, "is going to *disappear?*"

"I thought it was the gingerbread house that disappeared in your dream?"

"Well, yes. But if that goes, and Chester goes . . . I mean, we're sort of linked, you see."

"Whatever. This cake is seriously good." Mary paused in her eating. "It's a cool playhouse, by the way."

Mary was wrong, Stella decided, remembering that her interpretation of Jade O'Leary's money dream hadn't been entirely accurate. Chester's house wasn't going to disappear: how could it? With that comforting thought, Stella filled up Mary's glass. She was just reaching for the last strawberry tart before her guest could claim it, when voices from outside the playhouse made her stop in mid-reach. She cocked her head, listening. One voice was Chester's, but who was with him? A woman's voice . . .

Stella frowned, concentrating. Now she could hear their footsteps, which meant they'd reached the gravel path leading to *Stella Maris*. It wasn't like Chester to make unannounced calls. Tenants were entitled to their privacy, he'd said. He would enter the playhouse only if Stella was there and only if she invited him in.

"A playhouse!" exclaimed the woman. "I bet it has a million-dollar view."

Stella gasped. It couldn't be . . .

"What's the matter?" Mary asked.

"Ssshh!" Stella put a finger to her lips and tip-toed to the window. Flattening herself against the wall, she pulled back the batik curtain a little and peeped out. She couldn't see the speakers but she could hear them. Chester was saying something about "the rights of the tenant."

The woman laughed. "A tenant? In a play-house?"

"She's entertaining a friend at the moment. I don't like to disturb her, but since you're here—"

Feet crunched across the gravel and then mounted the ladder. "Watch out for the cat," Chester said.

Stella twitched the curtain back in place, her mind whirling. How on earth had this happened? What was she going to say? She could hardly pre-tend she wasn't in. Or could she? "Mary," she might say, "would you please answer the door and pretend I'm not here? I'll be hiding in the window seat." But there was no time. Mary would want to know why, and Chester would ask where she had gone and first she'd have to take out all the stuff that was in the window seat . . .

Footsteps crossed the balcony. There was a tap on the door.

"Oh, it's called *Stella Maris*. How sweet! My daughter's name is Stella."

"What a coincidence," Chester said. "My tenant's name is Stella." He tapped again on the door. "Stella, can I see you for a moment?"

There was nothing for it. She took a deep breath and opened the door.

"Hello, Chester. Hello, Mom."

"*Stella?*"

Of the two people at her door, it was hard to say who was the more astonished, but Lucille recovered faster. "What on earth are you doing here, Stella?" she exclaimed, staring at her daughter in surprise.

She could very well ask her mother the same question, Stella thought. Except she had a horrible feeling she already knew the answer. "Remember the friend with the big house by the sea I told you about," she began, but her mother had already put two and two together.

"So this is where you've been disappearing to all these weeks. Why didn't you say so?" She pushed past her daughter and stepped inside the playhouse. Her gaze rested on Mary, sitting at the table and enjoying the last of the lemon sponge cake. She smiled kindly. "And you must be Chessie."

"No," said Mary through a mouthful of crumbs. "I'm Mary Sparkel."

"*This* is Chessie . . . um, Chester," said Stella, turning to him. "Chester Vizard."

Lucille stared at him. "*You're* Chessie? I thought Chessie was Stella's friend."

81

"I am," said Chester. "That is, I'm her landlord, too. But I had no idea you were her mother." He turned to Stella. "Why didn't you tell me your mother was Lucille, the real-estate agent?"

"Because you said you hated real-estate agents and she was the worst and she was always pestering you to sell your house."

Chester gave a sort of spluttery cough and his face went red.

"I've never pestered anybody in my life," Lucille said frostily. "My job is to bring vendor and buyer together, not to pester. I called personally because none of my letters seemed to be getting through. Anyway, young lady, why didn't you tell me you were renting a playhouse?"

"I wanted a private place of my own," Stella said, not quite answering the question. "I saw this playhouse for sale but there was nowhere at home to put it so Chester agreed to rent it to me. We've got a contract and everything."

"She was very professional about the whole business," Chester said. "She's obviously learnt a lot from you."

Some of Lucille's frostiness melted. "I did give her some advice about short-term rentals. I just don't understand why she kept it a secret. Stella?"

Now they were both looking at her. Chester wanted to know the answer to that question, too. It had obviously never occurred to him that she hadn't told her parents about their arrangement. "I thought if I told you—" she began. Then she stopped. She wasn't the only one who had kept certain things secret. "Just a minute. Mom, if you didn't know I was Chester's tenant and Chester didn't know you were my mother, then what are you doing here? Chester's not interested in selling his house."

"He certainly is," Lucille said. She tapped her briefcase. "I've got the papers right here. We've been discussing the details all week."

"I told you those closing gates meant bad news," Mary said.

Stella shot her a furious look. How could she sit there calmly eating cake while Stella's dream collapsed around her?

"It's not really bad news," Chester said. "I wanted it to be a surprise—"

"A surprise?" Stella squeaked. "It's certainly a surprise. You told me only two months ago that you wouldn't sell. You said you weren't even *thinking* of selling."

"Mr. Vizard had the sense to realize that offers like this don't come along every day," her mother said.

"What offer?" Stella blinked angrily, trying to keep the tears at bay.

"I said I wouldn't sell *unless*..." Chester reminded her. "Stella, I've been offered a million-dollar deal. Who would have believed it? This old place!"

Lucille beamed. "This is prime beach frontage ripe for redevelopment. My client's going to build more townhouses."

"How could I refuse?" Chester said. "Especially when I was offered one as part of the sale."

"It's a sensational deal," her mother said. Chester nodded. Both of them looked as pleased as punch. Well, it was all right for them, Stella thought.

"Your house is going to be pulled down and my playhouse will have to go and you'll be living in a townhouse and you think it's a sensational deal?"

"Does anyone want this last strawberry tart?" asked Mary, reaching for it.

Stella had never been an emotional child, even given that so far there had been few events in her life to be emotional about. Her usual method of coping with setbacks was to shrug her shoulders and get on with life: if one door closed, another was sure to open. But now the disappointment was simply too crushing. She looked at the beaming faces of her mother and her landlord and at Mary Sparkel, Dream Expert, calmly munching her way through the remains of afternoon tea, all three of them seemingly indifferent to the fact that she, Stella, was about to lose her heart's desire. Something snapped inside her.

"How can you be so greedy?" she cried. "Yes, all three of you! Chester's greedy for money and Mom's only thinking of her agent's commission and Mary hasn't stopped stuffing her face since she sat down. All I wanted was a little house of my own and now it's going to disappear just like in my dream and not one of you cares." She burst into tears.

The three of them stared at her in surprise.

Chester cleared his throat. "I think a cup of tea

and a sticky bun might be a good idea at this point. Shall we adjourn to my kitchen?"

Stella glanced at the plans spread across the table but found it hard to summon any real interest in a proposal that spelled the end of *Stella Maris*. But Chester was clearly expecting a reaction of some sort, so she said, "You'll have a sea view, Chester."

He beamed. "That's one thing this old place doesn't have."

"You'll lose your big backyard though."

He shrugged. "I'm getting too old to look after this place, Stella. Sooner or later I'd have had to sell and someone would have shoved me into a retirement home. This way, I get to stay in Florence Street." He turned to Lucille. "Did I mention that it was Stella who introduced me to my neighbors? We're quite a friendly little bunch."

"I've always said that cluster living means companionship," Lucille said.

"Plus I'll have enough money to live on," Chester said. "I'm not getting any younger, you know. It's a very good outcome for me."

Stella tried to feel happy for him. Who was she to say that Chester should have turned down a million-dollar deal and a brand new Mediterranean townhouse with a view of the sea? *She* much preferred his gingerbread house, but she wasn't elderly and living on a pension; she didn't have to mow the lawn and weed the garden and trim the shrubs and repair the roof when it leaked and all the hundred and one things that needed doing around an old house. You couldn't afford to be sentimental when it came to selling a house; she'd told Chester that herself. Stella blew her nose. "I'm sorry I said you were greedy, Chester. Of course you've got to think of your future. And living here with Melissa and Marcel and Shane and

Jeffrey and Mr. Lee and Mrs. Adey will be much nicer than living in a retirement home."

Lucille looked puzzled and gazed around the kitchen as if she suspected all these people might be hiding in the cupboards.

"And Mom's just doing her job. Sorry I said you were greedy, Mom."

Lucille patted her hand. "You'll make a good real-estate agent one day, sweetie."

"When would you like me to move out?" Stella asked in a brave voice.

"Move out?" said Chester. "Stella, take a closer look. What do you think that is?" On the plan he pointed to what would be his new townhouse.

"Mr. Vizard made it very clear right from the word go that his tenant also had to be accommodated," Lucille said. She laughed. "I thought he meant a granny apartment."

Stella looked at the plan more carefully, hope

blossoming in her heart. A cluster of two-storey Mediterranean townhouses, linked with gardens and paving to the ones fronting Florence Street, all with courtyards and balconies and sea views, and the corner one—Chester's—with a little square box fronting the sandhills.

"That's *Stella Maris*," Chester said. "We'll plant some trees and vines. It'll be very private."

"Henry can help with that," Lucille said.

"You mean I can stay?" Stella exclaimed, so thrilled and relieved that not even the thought of Henry's landscaping bothered her.

"For as long as you like," Chester said. "I've got used to having you around. And who'd walk the dogs if you left?"

"What dogs?" Lucille asked.

Stella grinned. "I've got three dogs now, Mom. And a cat." She reached down and stroked Blackie, who was rubbing against her legs.

Lucille clucked her tongue. "I must say that seems rather greedy, Stella. Not many landlords would put up with all those pets."

"Not many landlords would feed you so well either," Mary Sparkel said, with a meaningful look. "It's like a dream come true, isn't it, Stella?"

Stella felt a stab of remorse. How could she have been so rude to a guest? Especially one as talented as Mary Sparkel. She was worth a hundred strawberry tarts. "I'm sorry I said you were greedy, Mary. I didn't mean it. And you're the best dream decoder in the entire world."

"I know."

"Just one little correction." Blackie jumped into her lap and purred, and Stella laughed with pure happiness. "Chester's a chef, just like you said, but he's definitely a wizard too."

"Whatever," said Mary Sparkel. "Does anyone want this last sticky bun?"

About Ruth Starke

The idea for this story came through watching those "backyard makeover" TV programmes. I usually prefer the original backyards to the new and "improved" versions, and I'm always very glad that nobody landscaped the backyard I had when I was growing up. It was large and rambling, with trees to climb, an old shed to hide in, and plenty of space in which to ride my bike, bash a ball about, and keep pets. (I had a dog, a magpie, a tortoise, and ducks.) Today in Australia, backyards like that are disappearing, which is sad.

I never had a proper playhouse, but the neighbors did. The two daughters of the family were grown up, so the playhouse belonged to the youngest child, Terry—a boy! What a waste, I thought, but in fact, Terry was as artistic as he was generous, and the two of us spent long glorious days decorating and playing in it.

What would I have done if I hadn't had that space and that playhouse? I like to write about kids who solve their own problems, like Lan in *NIPS XI*, who puts a whole cricket team together, or Sim in *Saving Saddler Street*, who battles to rescue his school from closure. I like to think I would have been as resourceful as Stella!